Happy Birthday (April 13)
Bishop Saunders -
Please enjoy these
humble writings of mine
Russell E. McDonald
04/09/00
410 433 8630

THE WAILS OF PALM TREES

Poetry And Other Writings

by
Rupel E. Marshall, Sr.

American Literary Press, Inc.
Baltimore, Maryland

The Wails of Palm Trees
Poetry and Other Writings

For permission and information write:
Rupel E. Marshall, Sr., 6 E. Lake Ave., Baltimore, MD 21212.

Cover Design: Sweeney, Inc.

Typesetting and Layout: Rupel E. Marshall, Sr.

Library of Congress
Cataloging in Publication Data
ISBN 1-56167-460-5

Published by

American Literary Press, Inc.
8019 Belair Road, Suite 10
Baltimore, Maryland 21236

Manufactured in the United States of America

First Printing: 1999

Paperback: $8.95

Dedication

To Rupel, Robert, Frederick, and Daniel whose lives and love soothe my tired mind.

The author's four sons: Rupel (right back), Robert (left back), Frederick (left front), and Daniel on the front steps to the home of Mrs. Joyce Johnson, Freetown, Sierra Leone, 1991. Mrs. Johnson provided free shelter in her home for the author and his family and for about thirty other Liberian refugees for over a year.

Acknowledgments

For the moral, financial, and technical supports given me to continue my writings and then to publish what I write, I am thankful to many persons. Some were involved directly, others indirectly; some knowingly; others unintentionally. And still others (K. Neville Best, Doughba Carmo Caranda II, Charles Neal II, and William B. Harris) encouraged me by examples; publication of their works provided me a level of confidence.

I thought I had "written," then Margaret, an excellent and encouraging writing instructor, would say, "Rupel you have to write." Professor Giron of Montgomery College came along at a different time and under a different circumstance (tutoring me in the honors humanities program) and said "revise, revise." Margaret made it clear that she could not advise on poetry but did find poesy in some of my writings. Thus, I included two of my speeches that were written like poems.

The lack of funds posed a challenge to the moral and technical support I received. I had to go up to several persons and say, "Please help me print my book." Thelma Traub Awori, Yvette Chesson-Wureh, Emmanuel J. Wureh, and Olive Mai Dennis responded favorably as soon as they were asked. I woke up many mornings wide-eyed: "When will I show these donors the results of the confidence they placed in me?" Pre-purchasing was next used to keep the writing and planning processes going. I am thankful to Evelyn Garnett, Josephine Desayou, Omolara Marshall, Joseph

Asante, Jim Johnson, Jonetta Singleton, Hawa Kpapah, and Efe Acosta for purchasing in the blind.

I was also encouraged to publish by the frequent requests and suggestions of various persons who heard me give a speech or read one of my poems. They also called on me to make presentations at public events which they were a part of, and that I felt honored playing a role. Some of these persons are the Rev. Michael Mattar, Ambassador Eugenia Stevenson, Edith Bright, Miatta Hoff, Counselor Joseph Williamson, Robert Gibson, the Rev. Sarah Perry, and Mother Anna Kamara. At times I felt like a bard. Other times I blushed as my works evoked laughters, smiles, and applause from audiences.

Mr. Latif Abdullah read one of my poems and remarked, "This stuff should be out there." He flowered his statement with offers of his home as a work site, his equipment, transportation, his time, technical help and a friendly disposition. Thank you Brother Latif and Family.

I am indeed thankful to my son Frederick for struggling to produce an artwork for the front cover. In this matter an effort was noble. Mrs. Peggy Cooper Caranda of Sweeney, Inc. finally came up with the one used on the front cover. I am also thankful to the following newspapers and bulletins that carried some of my works: *Catonsville Occupational Training Center News, W!tt, Gryphon* and *The Excalibur* of Montgomery College, Women Organized Resources for Liberia's Development, Inc. Newsletter, and the Liberian Christian Baptist Church Program Bulletin.

I am honored to have included in this humble endeavor of mine "The Sand Man," which received first prize in the 1997 *Write On* competition at Roland Park Elementary and Middle School in Baltimore, Maryland, through the permission of an upcoming poet, my youngest son, Daniel. I am equally honored by Mr. Carmo Doughba Caranda's professional assistance in providing the glossary, thus enabling the readers to grasp the depths of these writings.

In response to an Inner Voice and the encouragement so many gave me, I promise to continue to write, and to revise and revise, and, as now, to publish.

Contents

O*h*

Liberia!

We

Cry

For

Thee

Oh Liberia! We Cry For Thee

***O**h* Liberia! We cry for thee.
From day to day, we toss and weep.
Oh Liberia! Land of the free,
Gone are the nights of perfect sleep.

Young warriors by the hundreds came,
Knives dripped with blood in every hand.
They set our great nation aflame,
Man, woman, and child fled the land.

Brothers against brothers fighting,
People dying! Blood all around.
Guns roll and thunder like lightning,
Desecrating this hallowed ground.

Why does the Lone Star bleed this way?
The country floundered without love?
Some crime or sin of yesterday?
This a requital from above?

Must we not stop this bitter war
And bring these battles to an end?
Uniting behind the Lone Star,
Foes becoming friends among friends.

Only then we'll be free of pain,
No more strapped in greed, hate, or fear.
Free to build our nation again,
Couched in peace and freedom so dear.

Oh Liberia! We cry for thee
From day to day, we toss and weep.
Oh Liberia! Land of the free,
Gone are the nights of perfect sleep.

A Liberian refugee unexpectedly raised the Liberian flag as he and other refugees boarded a vessel in Freetown, Sierra Leone to return to Liberia, 1991. There were spontaneous outbursts of nostalgic joy, full of tears and clapping of hands when the flag suddenly unfolded.

Refugee

Refugee...
Roofed under leaves, in tents, in high-rises in America,
Omnipresent, even in the belly of Africa.

Refugee...
Stripped from family, friends, and home,
A battered stranger to distant lands I've come.
Those who never had to run do not understand,
Why in haste I had to flee the motherland.

Refugee...
This ID makes me a mockery to some I love.
But hate and revenge I will not prove.

Refugee...
Faith is my shield in this cultural crossfire.
Hope my strange accent does not keep me from hire
As I hold on to life and seek an honest job—
A surety that no man my dignity can rob.

Refugee...
Though in dismal conditions I now live
To reclaim my name I constantly strive.

Refugee...
Uneasy for my countrymen left behind,
In their rescue I will rest my tired mind.
And seek the demise of war, greed, and hate,
The chains that tie me to this ugly fate.

Come Leader Come

Oh come! Leader come!
God's commanding call: Rise up!
Sprout from beneath fear.

The guns — flash, thunder
Hunger, death, too much too long.
Corpses — dead flowers

Sing your native song,
Shout: *All hail, Liberia hail!*
End the wails of palm trees.

Introduction Of The Rev. J. Samuel Reeves

Those familiar
With the varying responses
Given two thousand years ago to the questions:
Who do men say I am?
And
Who do you say that I am?
Please empathize with me on
The shortfalls of this introduction of our
Distinguished Guest Speaker.

Our Guest Speaker,
A storehouse of knowledge and experience,
Through his writings, sermons, radio and television
appearances,
His counseling and his daily living,
Makes as his vocation,
A call to *Whosoever Will*
In the manner of the woman at Jacob's well
And in her words
To *Come See A Man.*

He,
As the pepperbird does early in the morning,

And, like the drumming sound of the *Dukpa* —
Liberia's talking drum —
Awakes Liberians from a slumber of loss and despair,
Onto a dawn of verdant light.

Such a message he brings tonight.

We Liberians say
A message is not a *kinjah*.
And, indeed, he beams with joy to bear us one.

As we gravitate to hear our Guest Speaker
Some are on edge
To hear what universities he attended —
And prestigious ones he did attend.
What degrees he has —
And high ones he earned.
All of this and more
Can be found in one of his many books entitled
So This Is Africa.

But the highest testimony
Of our Guest Speaker
And what we think of him
Come from a telephone call I received
At midnight two weeks ago.

The caller said to me,
"Our Guest Speaker is no 'small potato.'
When he served as chaplain of the Liberian army
Many soldiers were converted."
The caller provided me a measure of evidence.
She said,
"I saw many soldiers with little bibles."

Who knows
Whether a soldier refused
To pull the trigger of his gun at some innocent person
Thus, that person is spared
An early and unmarked grave;
And will this 26,
Back in Liberia,
Enjoy his Gbassajama,
His *Jallof Rice,*
His *Palava Sauce*
Or
Torborgee
And dance to the tunes of
All for You,
Baby Hold Me Tight,
Cousin Mosquito,
Jebe ina'a fesa,
Rocky Chu Chu,

And my favorite
Sio Lele, Sio Le?

Who knows
What properties remain intact
And some will return home
To once more
Enjoy their honest life's investments?

Or, who knows
That a man who will be found
Reclining in his hammock,
Under his *palaver* hut,
Showing off his *Vai* Shirt, *Tie Dye* Shirt
Or *Country Cloth* Gown;

Or, is it known
Whether a girl
Who this 26
Will shake her *sassa,*
Blush with earth decoratively splashed on her gyrating
  body
And will dance
Under the soothing tropical heat
Through the dusty streets
And village squares of Liberia.

Or, does anyone know
That a young person aged and weary by war
Will briskly share the Liberian handshake snap,
Test his *root bottle,*
Or, just sip *palm wine* or raw C. J.
While roasting an assortment of meat
on his broken coal pot,

Because
our Guest Speaker
Boldly and freely
Told the *Good News* to Soldiers in Liberia?

Such is a possibility.

I therefore ask you to rise.
Clap your hands
And receive a Liberian *Big Potato*:
The distinguished
Rev J. Samuel Reeves,
Guest Speaker.

The author with his sons Daniel (in his arm) and Frederick, waiting for food rations at a refugee distribution center in Freetown, Sierra Leone, 1991.

Between A Rock And No Place

We the Liberians
Returning home today from Sierra Leone
Aboard the ferry *Ile de Carabane*
Are 673 persons.
We left Freetown 4:35 P.M.,
Wednesday, June 12, 1991.
Captain Carl Carston captained
This vessel of voluntary returnees.

Thanks to Captain Carston and the crew
For the cool cruising and caring voyage.

The voyage
Was arranged by the *Liberian Council of Churches*
Through the sainted leadership of The Rev. Dr.
William N. Dixon.
The Council met the cost,
Commissioned me to bring our people home,
And the Council will continue this mission.

We salute our Sierra Leonean hosts,
The UN agencies,
Sierra Leonean Red Cross,
Lutheran World Services,

Catholic Relief;
Feed My People International, Cause Canada, CARE,
MSF, Etc.

Although our Sierra Leonean hosts were humane,
They are being attacked at this time
By persons believed to be jumping our borders.
We are now suspects.
Caught between a rock and no place,
Such a circumstance led us home.

Liberians cried out to return home.
To reclaim selfless service.
To again listen to the pepperbird.
To respond to the sounds of the Dukpa.

My team
Did the feeding, cleaning, and caring:
Joseph P. Nathan,
Kendrick Sawyer,
Mary Snetter,
Roseline Doe,
MaCauley Paykue,
Cynthia Castro,
Lasana Kamara,
Cecil Barnes,

Mohamed Mabande.
Hurrah to them!

God, grant success to these efforts.
Protect these emergency repatriations.
Continue us in the service of the Liberian people.

I present to you
277 Children
191 Women
205 Men.

My

Life!

Such

A

Journey

As

That

Mythical

Rock

Liberian refugees residing under trees at the U.N. Refugee Camp at Waterloo a few miles outside Freetown, Sierra, Leone, 1991. Refugees were required to provide the local material for their shelter and then the U.N. would provide plastic roofing. Many females and elderly persons who were unable to cut or buy sticks and branches and to build the structures lived in the open under trees for many days until assisted by fellow Liberians or the then Sierra Leone branch of the Liberian Council of Churches headed by the Rev. Dr. William N. Dixon. The author served as volunteer consultant to the Council in Sierra Leone.

The Rock

My life!
Such a journey as that mythical rock.
My strength and determination to Sisyphus.
Like that rock, I did overcome each stumbling block.
And many times I did reach the mountain top.
When a child, I blossomed in love. And as a man,
Husband a queen. I rose. I served my country well.
At the top I did the best a mortal can.
But on reaching the top, to the bottom I fell.
Moving up has often come to mean moving around,
And each break of day quickly turns to night.
I reached the top and rolled back to the ground.
When my pathway seemed clear, then out goes the
  light.
But this time round, I'll hold God's hand.
By His grace, I'll rise and forever stand.

The Portrait Of A Blessed Woman

(A Song To MAMA)

Discerning the harshness of our world,
She ventures into a desolate field.
She kneels down to pray;
A stillness fills the air.
In this moment of eloquent silence,
She hears the *Inner Voice*
Loud and clear:

Blessed is the woman who loves,
For the cares of this world are hers.

Blessed is the woman who blossoms as a rose,
For her touch bears no thorns.

Blessed is the woman who is resolute but serene,
For hers is the strength of Esther the Queen.

Blessed is the woman who gives of herself,
For she is fulfilled.

Blessed is the woman who stoops to uplift someone,
For her sleep is as a babe.

Blessed is the woman who is faithful and patient,
"For her price is far above rubies."

Blessed is the woman who tells nor listens to a lie,
For she is *primus inter pares.*

Blessed is the woman who nurtures her
children to pray, to labor, and to wait,
For she enriches the world.

Blessed is the woman who shows
A child the wonders
Of whispers of leaves,
Of beauty of flowers, of roaring of waters,
Of swirling of winds, of sprouting of seeds,
Of stillness of nights, of barrenness of deserts,
Of depth of oceans, of coming of births,
For she carves a future of beauty, love, peace,
and hope for mankind.

Blessed is the woman who bears a smile,
For she soothes the troubled,
She lights some dark paths,
She lowers some high mountains,
She stills some rough seas,
She covers the innocent,
She is complete.

I

Will

Not

Falter

Serving

Mankind

Mrs. Rachel E. Marshall, a retired international civil servant (nursing executive) and humanitarian. Mother of author.

Daddy Was A Barefoot Doctor

Daddy was a barefoot doctor
He traveled just about everywhere
To lift anyone in need of care

Scalpeling with his heart of gold
He stopped the sick from turning cold

Daddy was a barefoot doctor
He kept wide open the clinic door
Healed the young, the old, the poor

Through service he found unending pleasure
His golden heart his richest treasure

Daddy was a barefoot doctor
One day he brushed his feet off earthly dust
Evidently you and I someday must

Now at rest with our great ancestors
In that place prepared by the *Doctor of Doctors*

Daddy was a barefoot doctor
He made sure that someday I'll play my part
By bequeathing me his golden heart

With that piece of gold in body and mind
I will not falter in serving mankind

The author in the County office, Montserrado County Administrative Building, Bensonville, Liberia. He served as Superintendent (County Executive) of Montserrado County from 1986 to 1991.

What Christmas Means To Me

To always be kind, loving and true

Being all that I am meant to be
That is what each Christmas means to me

Just to watch a child open his toy —
Share in his flashing moments of joy

Each Christmas is all about true love
As sung by the angels from above —
Herald all to do the best they can
Lasting peace on earth, goodwill to man

Christmas is hope to a troubled face
Christmas brightens many a dark place
Time to join loved ones in distant miles
Exchanging gifts and bundles of smiles

Christmas is to rejoice and to sing
Hymns of praise to the heavenly king

And to say Merry Christmas to you

I'll Cry Again

When you first left, I did not know
Your touch, your smile, I would forget
My heart numbed, blood missed its flow
My pulse ran low, my eyes grew wet
When you first left, I did not know
One would come, we're a perfect set
Alive once more! My heart aglow!
I'll cry again, with joy you bet

What Is A Poem

All alone,
My lover up and gone.

I wish to go slow,
you know.

Hide in a sanctuary of words.

Weave a spider's web
With my pen

And

Draw thoughts that leap
From the page and warm
Some bosom.

Kiss me goodbye
Before I die.

I thought to grow
A writer's Rose.

Vision of Love

(The Marriage of Roland and Miatta)

I see
The heavens open wide
Two hugged to the Lord's side

I see
Them being blessed from above
With a touch of eternal love

I see
Two vow to leave any other
He, "his father and his mother"

I see
Hues of joy all around
Seeds of love they have found
Gone are doubts and fears
True signs for lasting years

I see
A faithful and young bride
His joy, his help, his pride

I see
Two as eternal friends
Cause true love never ends

Big Black Man?

(Address to the Jury)

A BIG black man?

The act was quick
For the double pick!
Counsel says
The evidence is not clear.
The brother says
He was not there.

This event is dramatic nationwide,
Prompting everyone to take a side.
One nuthead said: *Do all you can,*
Just do not marry a black man.

I believe
No one should kill,
But some do snap
When they've had their fill.
Some have heard
The blonde was fooling around
Such stories you know abound.

Gal or fellow,
Brown or yellow,
Black or white,
Fooling around is just not right.

Barks of a thousand dogs from door to door
Can not raise the dead from a bloody floor.

The People's Princess

Di was a princess not an ange***l***
Insensitive, the press tortured D***i***
At midnight they chased her to her gra***v***e
Now at peace with the angels abov***e***
Adieu! Diana, Princess of Wale***s***.

The author, a patron of Montserrado County (Liberia) Sports Program, witnessing the basketball finals of the 1990 National Sports Meet with two of his sons, Rupel and Robert, immediately back of him. Montserrado won the championship.

Epistles To My Four Sons

It's poison — no news from a distant child.

Even fools shun the thoughts of other fools.

Life — a bride who will forsake a true mate.

The wise say Yes when saying No to fools.

Child, only a fool sees darkness in light.

2

Child, comprehend life's writings on the wall;
Those who blink nor heed them are sure to fall.

Life is like my native fruit, *bitter sweet,*
Its sweetness is found in the bitter taste.

Child, life is a journey along blind curves,
Thus guard the haste of your eager nerves.

Know that a child's silence is refusal;
That of an adult is surely a crime.

No ugly rose stands even in the wild.
So too, God has not made a stupid child.

Child, true intentions need not be spoken,
But a false vow will surely be broken.

3

I ask of you this special deed:
To pray, to labor, and to wait.
Were you this humble call to heed,
The world would be yours — all of it.

Child, the noble deeds of famous men
Were borne through skill, labor and prayer.
Each stoop, an upward look to heaven.
Each action under-girded with care.

Don't bother a mortal who's hungry
Little else I think makes him angry.
First go give the poor soul some food,
Then in time your mission you may try.

Simone

A few months ago we met
You were a tiny bundle of life
Shamelessly smiling in diapers wet
Cuddled in your mother's arm
You pierced me with your charm

Now here you are crawling around
Still innocent but venturing
Gathering dirt from the ground

I am sure the next time we meet
You'll be a beauty with steady feet

Or, were we never again to see
I give this poem as a token of my love
A wish of what your future must be

Simone, I wish early in your youth
Someone will place and light in you
Three candles of *Love, Labor,* and *Truth*

Take them wherever you go, dear child
They'll protect, sustain, and comfort you
Through the valley, the calm, and the wild

Planted deep within, have no doubt
They'll glow forever around you —
No man nor element can put them out

Appendices

The Sand Man

The sand man comes from far away
Above the moon where the stars stay.
He found me in bed not asleep,
So he did his nightly job there —
Singing lullabies in the air,
Sprinkling dark sand over my eyes
Which he gathered from shining skies.
Softly down I went fast asleep
Quietly as a little sheep.

"The Sand Man," written by the author's youngest son, Daniel, then a nine-year-old fourth grader, won first prize in the 1997 *Write On* competition at Roland Park Elementary and Middle School in Baltimore, Maryland. It was first published in the June 1997 edition of *The Hudson Monthly.*

Liberian Folk Songs Mentioned

All For You
Baby Hold Me Tight
Cousin Mosquito
Jebe Ina'a Fesa
Rocky Chu Chu
Sio Lele, Sio Le

Liberian Dishes Mentioned

Jollof Rice
Torborgee
Palava Sauce
Gbassajama

Liberian Alcoholic Beverages Mentioned

Cane Juice (C.J.)
Palm Wine

List of Photographs

Glossary

Big Potato
Collaq, a very important person, usually with political clout.

Coal Pot
A locally made portable metal stove that uses charcoal for fuel. The stove is designed with a hollow top and legs. The coal is put on the top. Most coal pots are designed for one pot, but others can carry two or three pots.

Come See A Man
The call of the woman of Samaria to the villagers of Saycher as she ran from Jacob's well upon encountering Jesus Christ. (John 6:29)

Country Cloth
An indigenous cloth woven by hand from locally grown cotton. Weaving is usually done by a male who uses a customized wooden scaffold to weave the cloth. Special dye, made from the bark of trees, is used to give color to the natural white cotton. The woven material represents honor and royalty.

Dixon, William N.
Liberian humanitarian and religious leader, founder and chairman of the Liberian School for the Deaf. He spearheaded the relief assistance and repatriation of thousands of Liberian refugees from Sierra Leone to Liberia when conditions got too desperate for them in Sierra Leone during the Liberian civil war.

Dukpa
A traditional talking drum used to produce special sounds

that communicate specific messages. It is popular among the Bassa tribe of Liberia.

Good News
The teachings of Jesus Christ.

Kinjah
A semi-oval-shaped container made of fresh palm branches, platted together and padded with leaves for the purpose of carrying produce from the farm to the market or home. The items are well packed so that much can be carried in the kinjah. When the kinjah is filled, leaves are placed over the items and the kinjah is tied with a rope. The value of the kinjah is that when a farmer or an individual goes to get what he desires to bring to town, he does not have to take a container with him. The kinjah is made on site from readily available material such as leaves, branches, and rope made from vines. The kinjah, when ready to carry, is referred to as a load, which it is. Thus, Liberians are usually heard saying "a message is not a kinjah," meaning one bears no burden or responsibility for delivering a message.

Liberia
A republic of West Africa bounded by the Atlantic Ocean, Sierra Leone, the Ivory Coast, and Guinea. It was founded in the early 1800s by freed blacks from the United States. In December 1989, a civil war erupted that lasted for seven years, leaving at least 200,000 persons dead and about 800,000 exiled as refugees. The population before the war was put at 2.5 million.

Liberian handshake snap
A manner of greeting peculiar to Liberians. The shake is made by presenting the right hand to the other person upon meeting. Once the hands are engaged, the thumb and third

finger of both hands are lightly snapped as the hands disengage, making a sound.

Lone Star
The Liberian flag because it has a single star on it. The national soccer team is also called the Lone Star.

Palavar Hut
A usually wall less veranda-like building of wooden poles and mud, roofed with thatch. It has two or three entrances. It serves as a small court house where the elder(s) or chief(s) settle grievances of the villagers. It is also used as a relaxing place away from the main house.

Palm Tree
One of the oldest families of the plant world, it is found in most tropical regions of the world. There are many species. The Elaeis genuineness is native to Africa. Most palm trees grow tall and straight and the branches droop off the side except for the top. It bears a reddish orange fruit called the palm nut. The palm nuts can be prepared into an assortment of food, and it and other parts of the tree can be used for fuel, cosmetics, oil, medicine, signs, decorations, furniture, alcoholic beverages, etc.

Pepperbird
A beautiful bird considered indigenous to Liberia. It eats small pods of pepper, thus its name. It sings early in the morning serving as an alarm clock that it is time to start the day's activities.

Reeves, J. Samuel
A Liberian pastor of Whoseoever Will Baptist Church in Wheaton, Maryland, USA and host of a television program in the same state. He is a former chaplain of the Liberian

Army, former legislator, and an educator.

Root Bottle
Any bottle containing selected roots, herbs, nuts, fruits and liquor. This concoction is drunk as a delicacy, a laxative, remedy to various sexual problems, the common cold, etc. The preferred liquor is the locally brewed cane juice from sugar cane plant. Men cherish their root bottles and offer a drink from it only to special guests and good friends.

Sassa
A musical instrument that has a distinctive sound. It is constructed by selecting a smooth gourd and placing it in a net-like sac strung with beads, seeds, rattles or buttons. The strings are usually made of cotton thread for maximum shaking and tension playing. The manner of holding the sassa makes a difference regarding the musical effects and a creative statement. Both men and women play the sassa, but traditionally women play it the most.

Sierra Leone
A West Africa nation on the east of Liberia.

Sisyphus
Legendary ruler of Corinth punished in Tarlarus by being compelled to roll a rock to the top of a hill. The rock always rolled back down. He starts the task over each time.

Small Potato
An ordinary person who thinks he is important or has influence when he has none.

Vai Shirt
A collarless short sleeve shirt with three front pockets (one on the upper chest and two lower ones). It is popular among

the Vai tribe of Liberia, thus its name.

Whosoever Will
Jesus Christ's command for all to freely accept salvation (Mark 8:34).

Order Form

Permission is granted to copy this order form.

To order additional copies of *The Wails of Palm Trees and Other Writings*, provide the below information:

Ship to: (Please print)

Name: ______________________________

Street Address: ______________________________

City, State, Zip: ______________________________

Day Phone: ______________________________

Please send me ______ copies at $8.95 each. $ ________

Include $2.50 postage and handling/each book $________

Total enclosed $________

Make check or money order payable to:

Rupel E. Marshall, Sr.

Send to:

Rupel E. Marshall, Sr.

6 E. Lake Avenue

Baltimore, MD 21212

The Wails of Palm Trees and Other Writings makes excellent reading for entertainment, relaxation, meditation and reflection. It is also a great gift item for holidays, birthdays, anniversaries, graduations, or for someone recovering from an illness. It is also recommended for young readers.